my little Pony

Phonics
Fun

I Can Read Book® is a trademark of HarperCollins Publishers.
My Little Pony: *Pony Friends*
My Little Pony: *A Bad Nap*
My Little Pony: *Get Set for Fun!*
My Little Pony: *Bad Luck, Good Luck*
My Little Pony: *The Big Fair*
My Little Pony: *The Hot Day*
My Little Pony: *Cotton Candy's Band*
My Little Pony: *A New Friend*
My Little Pony: *Pony Fun*
My Little Pony: *The Pony Picnic*
My Little Pony: *A Letter from a Friend*
My Little Pony: *Pony Party*

Stories by Joanne Mattern
Phonics scope and sequence developed by
Cathy Toohey, Educational Consultant

First Edition

11 12 13 14 15 SCP 10 9 8 7 6 5 4 3 2 1

my little Pony

Phonics Fun

TABLE OF CONTENTS

Letter to Parents

Dear Parents,

Welcome to the I Can Read! phonics program. Your child is about to start an exciting adventure. He or she is going to learn to read. By choosing your child's favorite characters, you have already accomplished something very important: motivation!

My Little Pony Phonics Fun includes twelve storybooks, planned by a phonics expert. The books are intended for children to read at home with a parent or caregiver and, eventually, by themselves.

- *My Little Pony Phonics Fun* introduces the short vowel sounds *a, e, i, o,* and *u.* One of the key components in becoming a fluent reader is practice, so this set features two books for each sound, plus one introductory story, and one book that reinforces all the sounds. Learning to read short vowels is rewarding because they are found everywhere!
- Fun *My Little Pony* words have been included to make the stories rich and enjoyable.
- The stories also include sight words. These are words frequently found in books that can be hard to sound out. They just need to be learned by sight!
- Picture clues support the text in each story and help children learn new words.

As children master the sounds and words, they will gain experience and confidence in their ability to understand sounds, sound out words, and READ! Here are some suggestions for using *My Little Pony Phonics Fun* to help your child on the road to reading:

1. Read the books aloud to your child. The first time you read a story, read it all the way through. Then invite your child to follow along by pointing out words as you read them. Encourage him or her to try to sound out new words that use familiar sounds, or that are pictured in the illustrations.

2. Discuss each sound found on the first page with your child. Help your child sound out the new words in the story. Demonstrate the vowel sounds— for example, by telling your child that the short **o** vowel sound is found in the word **hot**.

3. Look at the pictures with your child. Encourage him or her to tell the story through the pictures. Point out objects in the pictures and ask your child to name them.

We hope that you and your child enjoy *My Little Pony Phonics Fun,* and that it is the start of many happy reading adventures.

The HarperCollins Editors

my little Pony

BOOK **1**
Introduction

Pony Friends

In this story you will learn new sight words.
Can you find these words?

my   **like**   **all**

is   **a**

I   **we**

Here are some fun My Little Pony words:

name   **pony**   **pink**

meet   **friends**

Hello! My name is Minty.

Let's meet my pony friends.

This is Sunny Daze.

I like Sunny Daze.

Hello, Sparkleworks!

Sparkleworks is my friend.

Here is a pony friend.

She is Pinkie Pie!

Hello, Pinkie Pie!

Here is a pink pony.

I like pink ponies!

This pony is Skywishes.

I like my pony friends.

And we all like you!

my little Pony

BOOK 2
Short a

A Bad Nap

In this story you will learn about the **short a** vowel sound. Can you find these words and sound them out?

nap   had   bad   ran   can

Here are some fun My Little Pony words:

sleepy   dream   away

Here are some new sight words:

she   the   go
saw   make   said

Pinkie Pie was sleepy.

Pinkie Pie took a nap.

Pinkie Pie had a bad dream.

She saw a bad monster.

Pinkie Pie ran. She ran away from the bad monster.

Rainbow Dash woke her friend.
"I can help!" she said.

Pinkie Pie told her friend
her bad dream.

"Friends can make
bad dreams go away!"
said Pinkie Pie.

my little Pony

BOOK 3
Short e

Get Set for Fun!

In this story you will learn about the **short e** vowel sound. Can you find these words and sound them out?

let's   **wet**   **tent**   **went**

get   **dress**   **ten**

Here are some fun My Little Pony words:

outside   **pretty**   **treats**

Here are some new sight words:

play   **to**   **they**   **what**

"Let's play,"
said Twinkle Twirl.
"Let's play outside."

"Let's get wet!"
said Skywishes.
She liked to get wet.

"Now let's play dress up!"
said Twinkle Twirl.
She put on a pretty dress.

Later the ponies set up
a small tent.

Then they ate ten treats.

"What a fun day!"
said the ponies.
And then they all went home.

I Can Read! Phonics

my little Pony

BOOK 4
Short u

Bad Luck, Good Luck

In this story you will learn about the **short u** vowel sound. Can you find these words and sound them out?

up   sun   fun   luck   but

Here are some fun My Little Pony words:

kite   fly   balloons

Here are some new sight words:

look   that

Skywishes has a kite.

Look at that!

Up goes the kite.

It goes up to the sun!

Kimono gets her kite.

The kites go up!

This is fun!

Bad luck!

The kites fly away.

Look at the balloons!
The balloons go up
to the sun.
This is fun!

Bad luck!

The balloons fly away.

"Kites and balloons fly up and away," said Skywishes. "But friends are forever!"

my little Pony

BOOK 5
Short i

The Big Fair

In this story you will learn about the **short i** vowel sound. Can you find these words and sound them out?

skipped   pick   kicked   it

big   slid   win   hit

Here are some fun My Little Pony words:

fair   slide   prize

Here are some new sight words:

down   do

The ponies skipped
down the road.
They skipped to the big fair.

"Let's pick a fun thing to do," said Rainbow Dash.

The ponies slid.

They slid down a slide.

They slid down fast!

Minty picked a game.

She kicked a ball.

"I win!" Minty said.

Minty picked a prize.

Sunny Daze went fast.

It was fun!

The big fair was a big hit!

BOOK 6
Short o

The Hot Day

In this story you will learn about the **short o** vowel sound. Can you find these words and sound them out?

hot **pop** **lot** **stopped** **not**

Here are some fun My Little Pony words:

beach **sand** **waterfall**

Here are some new sight words:

very **are** **of**

It was hot.

It was a very hot day.

The ponies were at the beach.

The sand was hot!

"I have an ice pop,"
said Skywishes.
"I like ice pops on hot days!"

The ponies went to the well.
They drank a lot of water.

Skywishes stopped
under a waterfall.
The water was not hot.

"Hot days are a lot of fun!"
said Skywishes.

BOOK 7
Short a

Cotton Candy's Band

In this story you will learn about the **short a** vowel sound.

Do you remember these words?

had   can

Can you find these words and sound them out?

plan   band   glad   sad   clapped

Here are some fun My Little Pony words:

start   sang   song   sing

Here are some new sight words:

wanted   don't   be   was

Cotton Candy had a plan.
She wanted to start a band.

The ponies were glad.

They liked Cotton Candy's plan.

Sunny Daze sang.

She sang a song.

Cotton Candy was sad.

She wanted to sing a song.

"Don't be sad," said the ponies. "All of us can sing a song."

Cotton Candy was glad.
Everyone clapped
for the band.

my little Pony

BOOK 8
Short e

A New Friend

In this story you will learn about the **short e** vowel sound.

Do you remember this word?

went

Can you find these words and sound them out?

spend   pet   bent   fed   best

Here are some fun My Little Pony words:

window   found   furry   friend

Here are some new sight words:

her   say   with   are

Daisy Jo went to
her window.

She found her pony friends.
"Let's spend the day outside!"
they said.

The ponies went for a walk.
"Look! A new furry friend!"
said Kimono.

"Let's pet the rabbit!"
said Daisy Jo.
Rainbow Dash bent down
to say hello.

Then the ponies went home
with their new friend.
They fed the rabbit.

"New friends are the best!"
said Rainbow Dash.

my little Pony

BOOK 9
Short u

Pony Fun

In this story you will learn about the **short u** vowel sound.

Do you remember these words?

fun up

Can you find these words and sound them out?

jumped drums spun hug

Here are some fun My Little Pony words:

stage danced nice

Here is a new sight word:

loved

The ponies had fun.

The ponies played dress up.

Rainbow Dash jumped up
on stage.
She loved her nice dress!

Minty played drums.

Toola Roola played drums,
too.

Then she spun around.

The ponies got up.

They jumped and danced.

Then they all shared
a big hug.

I Can Read! Phonics

my little Pony

BOOK 10
Short i

The Pony Picnic

In this story you will learn about the **short i** vowel sound.

Do you remember this word?

hit

Can you find these words and sound them out?

picnic will dish mix picks big

Here are some fun My Little Pony words:

stir tasty cupcakes

Here are some new sight words:

is today

Today is a good day
for the pony picnic.

Sweetberry will make
a nice dish.

What will she make?

Sweetberry and Cupcake stir.

Sweetberry and Cupcake mix.

Sweetberry makes tasty cupcakes.

She picks up the dish.

The pony picnic is a big hit!

BOOK 11
Short o

A Letter from a Friend

In this story you will learn about the **short o** vowel sound.

Do you remember this word?

not

Can you find these words and sound them out?

mailbox   **stop**   **lots**

got   **clock**   **lost**

Here are some fun My Little Pony words:

sleepover **party**

Here are some new sight words:

there **brought**

Every mailbox had a letter
in it from Cherry Blossom.

The letter said, "Come to my sleepover party!"
All the ponies got the letter.

"I must stop baking and take a nap," said Triple Treat. Then she went to sleep.

"I have got to set the clock," said Skywishes.

Then she took a nap, too.

There were lots of friends
at the party.
But not Skywishes.
Her clock had not rung.

But all was not lost.
The ponies brought the
party to Skywishes's house!

my little Pony

BOOK 12
Vowel Sounds

Pony Party

In this story you will review the vowel sounds. Can you find these words and sound them out?

big **wish** **ran** **best**

lots **fun** **jumped** **and**

Here are some fun My Little Pony words:

pony **baked** **cakes**

party **pies**

Do you remember these sight words?

today **a** **I** **so** **we**

was **she** **they** **said** **are**

Today was a big day.
Today was the day
of the pony party!

Sweetberry baked.

She baked pies.

She baked lots of cakes.

Skywishes made a wish.
"I wish for a fun party!"

The ponies played games.

They ran.

They jumped.

Then a butterfly came.

"It is so pretty!"

said Sparkleworks.

"This was the best party!"
said Twinkle Twirl.
"And we are best friends!"